THE MYSTERY of the LOST MAP

THE ADVENTURES OF
COWBOY LITTLE AND COWBOY SMALL

THE MYSTERY *of the* LOST MAP

JIM RHODEN
in collaboration with Mickey Goodman
Illustrations by Marilena Perilli

LANIER
PRESS

Alpharetta, GA

This is a work of fiction. Names, characters, businesses, places, and events are either the products of the author's imagination or are used in a fictitious manner. Any resemblance to actual persons, living or dead, or actual events is purely coincidental.

ISBN: 978-1-63183-353-3 - Paperback
ISBN: 978-1-63183-490-5 - Hardcover
eISBN: 978-1-63183-354-0 - ePub
eISBN: 978-1-63183-355-7 - Mobi

Library of Congress Control Number: 2018967228

Printed in the United States of America   1 2 1 4 1 8

∞This paper meets the requirements of ANSI/NISO Z39.48-1992 (Permanence of Paper)

Illustrations by Marilena Perilli

These stories about Cowboy Little and Cowboy Small are dedicated to my parents, Nelle and Lloyd Rhoden, who encouraged my independence as a young boy and gave me the freedom and self-confidence to explore the world around me.

I further dedicate this book to my children, Jay, Mitch, and Jodi, for constantly urging me to put these tales on paper. I am overjoyed that they consider my nightly bedtime stories among their best childhood memories.

And to my grandchildren, Shawn, Jasper, Henry, Raleigh, JR, Nora, Becca, and Mack. May these words prompt your curiosity and desire to explore.

Also to Sally, the mother of my children and a wonderful companion for many years. Thank you for your tolerance of my many tales and for continually encouraging my creativity.

To paraphrase the great James Michener:
"First, buy a cowboy hat and boots. Then you're on your
way to becoming a cowboy."

CONTENTS

ACKNOWLEDGMENTS

In addition to family members, thanks to the many people who encouraged me along the way, among them Jack Wilson, Judy Meadows, Ashley O'Neil, Patty Smitherman, and Ann J. Anderson.

I'd also like to thank my collaborator, Mickey Goodman, who was born in Chicago and never saw wide-open spaces until she moved to the South. Initially, she was stumped by my idioms and colloquialisms, but adapted quickly and well. Her "nudging" and contacts with the writing and publishing worlds have helped bring these writings to fruition.

Thanks, too, to our talented illustrator, Marilena Perilli, who captured the adventuresome spirits of Cowboy Little and Cowboy Small and brought them to life. A New Yorker who had never visited the West, she was a quick study whose drawings of landscapes and animals were both realistic and charming.

Last, I would like to give a sincere thank-you to our publishers at Lanier Press. Their entire team was always accommodating, even when I challenged their normally steadfast ways of following the protocol of the publishing world. A good example is my insistence that although the book is oriented for children 4–10, I wanted to include book lovers from 3–100. Age should never be a barrier to one's imagination or dreams!

A NOTE TO MY READERS

Hollywood cowboys—the Lone Ranger, Roy Rogers, Hopalong Cassidy, and Gene Autry—were a big part of my world when I was growing up. They were my heroes. In the movies, the good guys wore white cowboy hats and the bad guys always wore black hats. The good guys always caught the bad guys, and truth, honesty, and the American way won out over dirty deeds.

As my children grew up, the difference between the good and bad guys blurred. I wanted them to admire the white-hat heroes of the West that I remembered. So, I made up bedtime stories about Cowboy Little and Cowboy Small, their horses Ned and Ted, their dogs Red and Fred, their fleas Itch and Scratch, and their cattle Brawny Bull* and Helen Heifer.

The little cowboys in my stories were independent, adventuresome, brave, and resourceful—the way I wanted my children and grandchildren to be. They have far exceeded my expectations.

These tales were taken from my childhood, a different time and a different era when it was safe for kids to roam without supervision. At age nine or ten, I would get on my horse, Trigger, grab my rifle and my bedroll, and head out looking for adventure in the piney woods on the Phipps Plantation north of Tallahassee, Florida. Being allowed to roam freely afforded me the independence to make mistakes and figure out ways to correct them on my own.

My hope is that you and your children will take from these pages happy thoughts, laughter, and a sense of doing what's right just because it's the right thing to do.

*NOTE: Brawny Bull was originally named Horny Bull because of his six-foot-long horns. His name was changed at the insistence of my collaborator and editor.

Chapter 1

THE HUNT FOR ARROWHEADS

None of the students in the one-room schoolhouse were paying attention to the teacher as she wrote math problems on the blackboard. Instead, seventeen pairs of eyes stared at the ceiling, watching a narrow leak in the roof turn into a steady stream of rain that came splish-splashing onto the teacher's desk. It drenched the slates waiting to be graded. It soaked her history book. It even dripped off the shiny silver bell she rang everyday.

She turned to face the class just as the hole in the ceiling grew even bigger. Rain plopped on her head, dribbled down her face, and soaked her from top to bottom.

Then the giggling began.

"Oh, my goodness gracious," she gasped. "It's raining *inside*. I think we'll have to dismiss classes early."

Every student, from the youngest to the oldest, yelled, "Hip hip, hooray!" But none were louder than Cowboy Little and Cowboy Small, who whooped and hollered and threw their white cowboy hats in the air.

Cowboy Small, who was sitting near the front with the younger kids, jumped out of his chair and turned toward his brother. "We can leave early to look for arrowheads at Two Gulch Gap!" he yelled.

"Yay!" shouted Cowboy Little, who sat two rows back with the older kids. "Meet you at the horses. "

Before the teacher could even ring that shiny, wet silver bell, every single student ran out the red front door and headed home. They didn't even mind that it was raining hard or that they were getting wet. They were out early on a Friday afternoon, leaving more time for fun over the weekend.

Cowboy Little and Cowboy Small made a mad dash to the school corral, jumped on their horses Ned and Ted, and headed for the Circle R Ranch. That's where they lived with their Mama and Daddy, Grandma Hettie and Grandpa Jake, their brothers Cowboy Big and Cowboy Tall—all Randalls— and a passel of cowhands. They could hardly wait to see their dogs Red and Fred, their fleas Itch and Scratch, and their cattle Brawny Bull and Helen Heifer. Their pets went with them on all their adventures.

To Cowboy Little, his gentle and quick cow pony, Ned, was the most beautiful horse in the whole wide world. He had a light-brown back and a dark-blond mane and tail. Ned loved Cowboy Little as much as any horse could love a little cowboy, and Cowboy Little loved Ned as much as any boy could love a horse.

Ted, Cowboy Small's horse, was a big, rangy moose of a horse with a shaggy, rust-colored coat and a black mane and tail. Ted loved Cowboy Small as much as a horse could love a little cowboy, and Cowboy Small loved Ted as much as a little cowboy could love a horse.

Their dogs Red and Fred loved both boys and protected them from danger. They barked happily when they saw the boys and ran around them in circles. They sensed adventure in the air.

Red was the biggest with a coat that was bright orange-red like his name. Red especially loved the little cowboys because they had rescued him when he was a hungry, lost puppy. Fred was as black as midnight when there's no moon and the stars are turned off. He was smart, too, and helped the cowboys herd their cattle. He would bark a special warning if he sensed danger.

When they reached the ranch house, the boys burst into Mama's warm kitchen. They were hankering for some buttermilk and a slice of fresh apple pie.

"The teacher let us out early on account of it rained through a big hole in the roof," Cowboy Small said. "It dripped on her head and all over her desk!"

"Oh, dear me," said Mama. "I'm afraid the schoolhouse needs a new roof. But I bet you boys weren't too sad. Do you have big plans for the weekend?"

They grinned. "We're goin' on an adventure to look for arrowheads at Two Gulch Gap," said Cowboy Small. "I want to find one like Cowboy Little found when we were with Daddy awhile back."

"Well, before you go, don't forget to do your chores."

Cowboy Little sighed. "We better work fast so we kin leave before dark."

Living on a ranch was hard work, even for the youngest members of the family. Every day the boys had to chop big logs for the fireplace and enough small kindling for Mama's stove. Then they shucked a bag full of corn for the chickens, turkeys, Guinea hens, and peacocks. They cleaned out the horses' stalls and filled them with fresh hay. The last chore was sweeping the porch.

As soon as Mama and Daddy, Grandma Hettie, and Grandpa Jake were satisfied that all their chores were done, Mama packed their saddlebags with plenty of food and tied their bedrolls and rain slickers onto the backs of their saddles. The boys added their rifles and fishing poles.

"Good bye." Mama waved. "Be keerful. Watch out for snakes."

"Good bye," said Daddy. "Catch some big fish in Cripple Creek."

"Good bye," said Grandma Hettie. "Be keerful. Look out for bears."

"Good bye," said Grandpa Jake. "Have fun. I hope you find some arrowheads."

Except for Mama, who fretted a lot, the grownups weren't worried about the boys spending the night at Two Gulch Gap, just inside the North Forty on the edge of the ranch property. They had explored nearly all of the Circle R Ranch from sun up to sun down by themselves, and had proven they could take care of themselves.

Cowboy Little was a rugged, independent, and curious cowboy. Once when he was playing hide-and-seek, he climbed a tree so high that no one could find him. Another time, he killed a rattlesnake with a single shot from his rifle.

His brother, Cowboy Small, was so smart he could work really hard math problems in his head. Even though he was two years younger, he was a head taller than his brother. That made Cowboy Little jealous. Both loved adventures even better than helping break in the new ponies on the ranch.

By the time they set off for Cripple Creek Trail to Two Gulch Gap, the sun was beginning to slide behind the hills. But they weren't afraid. They had been on the trail a million times. So had their horses Ned and Ted, their dogs Red and Fred, their fleas Itch and Scratch, and their cattle Brawny Bull and Helen Heifer.

"Everybody ready?" asked Cowboy Little, looking back to make sure all the animals were following.

"Forward ho!" yelled Cowboy Small.

Chapter 2

DISCOVERY

They trotted down Cripple Creek Trail so they could get to Two Gulch Gap before it got too dark. On the way they saw a big mule deer with a huge rack of antlers and a red fox chasing a squirrel. And, right in the middle of the road, were two of the cutest bear cubs you ever could see.

"Uh-oh," said Cowboy Little. "That means mama bear is somewhere around, and we sure don't want to git between her and those cubs. That makes mama bears real, real mad."

"We gotta hightail it right on past them before mama bear knows we're even here," said Cowboy Little. With that, he slapped Ned on his flank and took off at a full gallop. Cowboy Small galloped close behind on Ted. Red and Fred scampered alongside. Brawny Bull snorted and Helen Heifer mooed as they circled around the bear cubs.

"We dodged a bullet," said Cowboy Small. "Even Brawny Bull woulda been no match for a mama bear protecting her cubs."

When Cowboy Little and Cowboy Small, their horses Ned

and Ted, their dogs Red and Fred, their fleas Itch and Scratch, and their cattle Brawny Bull and Helen Heifer reached Two Gulch Gap, they found a real mess. The fire-circle rocks had been scattered, and there was trash everywhere.

"I bet some sorry cowboys left food and junk behind and the raccoons found it," said Cowboy Little. "But why would anyone move the fire-circle rocks?"

"They must have been looking for somethin'," said Cowboy Small.

"Tell you what. I'll clean up this mess and make a fire. You catch us a fish for dinner in Cripple Creek," said Cowboy Little.

"Why, sure," said Cowboy Small. He grabbed his fishing pole and took off toward Cripple Creek before his brother could change his mind.

With the light cast by the full moon, Cowboy Small found some fat worms and grubs in the rotting logs to lure the fish. He tiptoed so he wouldn't spook the trout feeding near the edge. Then, he baited his hook and cast a large, juicy, black-and-gray worm upstream from a big ol' rainbow trout.

The current drifted the worm right over that smart old trout. But about the time Cowboy Small was ready to cast again, the wily trout grabbed that worm. He took off upstream as fast as his big, broad tail could push him.

Cowboy Small was a good and patient fisherman. When the trout pulled the line out as far as it would go, it twanged like a screechy guitar. He pulled that feisty fish around the fallen log and along the shallow water. With a flick of the pole like his brother Cowboy Tall had taught him, he had that rainbow-colored trout dangling from the end of his fishing pole. It was plenty big for the two of them for supper.

Back at the campsite, Cowboy Little picked up the trash and reset the fire pit. He was gathering firewood when he saw a pair of saddlebags peeking out behind two humongous rocks.

Cowboy Small came whistling up the hill, ready to brag about the size of the trout, but before he could say a word, Cowboy Little whooped. "Look at these old, worn-out saddlebags I found! It must have been one really dumb cowboy to leave them behind. Somethin' strange is goin' on at Two Gulch Gap."

The boys grinned at one another, the fish forgotten. There was nothing they liked better than solving a mystery. Cowboy Little put his bedroll on the ground and set the strange saddlebags on top. Then he carefully unbuckled the straps on the left saddlebag. First, he pulled out an oily rag wrapped around an old Army Colt .45 and gently put it on the blanket. Then he reached into the saddlebag again. Cowboy Small's eyes got as big as the full moon when his brother pulled out a pair of buckskin Indian moccasins.

They were old and frayed, but decorated with beads outlining an eagle in flight. "Grandpa Jake once told me the eagle is the mark of a powerful Hopi Indian chief," said Cowboy Small. "I wonder if these were made by the same Indian who lost the arrowhead I found when we were here the last time."

"Daddy says there's a Hopi Indian village in the valley. It's all very mysterious."

There was only one more thing in the left saddlebag: a leather pouch that jingled when Cowboy Little shook it. He turned it upside down on the blanket and a passel of gold coins fell out. Their mouths flew open. "We've found a treasure!" they yelled. "We're rich!"

They fingered the coins for a few minutes, then Cowboy Small said, "Let's see what's on the other side of the saddlebag. Maybe we'll find more gold coins."

The contents of the right saddlebag were even more mysterious. Out came a packet of letters and a large map. Next were the sort of things cowboys usually carried: a box of ammunition for the pistol and a small tin filled with fishing line, corks, and hooks. The very last thing was an old book with fancy decorations on the cover.

"On the front it says 'Kirschner's Medical Dictionary,'" said Cowboy Small. "But there are too many big words inside. The only thing I kin read is the date—1826. That was a long, long time ago."

Cowboy Little took one of the letters out of the envelope and tried to read it. The letters were so fragile that he was afraid of tearing them. He decided to wait for Mama's help.

The map, too, was very old. It had been folded and unfolded so many times, it was almost in pieces. But Cowboy Little and Cowboy Small couldn't resist. They carefully spread it out on the blanket near the light of the fire.

"What kind of crazy map is this?" asked Cowboy Small. "There are no straight lines or trails. There's only symbols of animals, crops, and mountain peaks . . . but lookee there. That squiggle might be a river."

"What's that yellow ball in the corner? Is that a sun? Or mabe the mark of a place where someone hid more gold coins?" asked Cowboy Little.

Neither knew the answer.

"Tomorrow we'll show it to Grandpa Jake," said Cowboy Small. "With the saddlebags bein' so old, there's no tellin' who they rightly belong to. But he's old and he knows everything. I bet he can fig'er it all out."

By that time, the fire pit was hot enough to cook the fish like Daddy had taught them. They flipped it over at the perfect time. For dessert, they had Mama's biscuits with sorghum syrup. Then they shared the leftovers with their dogs Red and Fred.

"Yum," said Cowboy Little, rubbing his tummy.

"Yum," said Cowboy Small. He looked at the starry sky and their animals grazing nearby. "We are the luckiest cowboys in the West."

After eating, they sat cross-legged near the fire pit and argued. "Where 'bouts are we gonna hide the saddlebags so they're safe while we sleep?"

"We could use them like pillows," said Cowboy Little.

"That's a dumb idea," said Cowboy Small. "Some sneaky cowhand could come along and take them away. Let's hide them under some brush near Cripple Creek."

Cowboy Little gave him a mean look. They fussed for a few minutes like brothers often do. In the end, they decided to hide the saddlebags in a small bat cave near the camp.

Cowboy Small added some more wood to the fire to keep them warm all night. Cowboy Little, who wasn't as afraid of bats as his brother, dragged the heavy saddlebags up the hill. He hid them behind a big rock inside the cave.

"What do all the things we found mean?" asked Cowboy Little. "We gotta head back to the Circle R at daylight to show everyone the treasure."

For once, Cowboy Small didn't argue.

The little cowboys used their saddles as pillows. They curled up under the stars as a soft evening song sung by the swift running waters of Cripple Creek lulled them to sleep. The next day would surely bring exciting adventures for Cowboy Little and Cowboy Small, their horses Ned and Ted, their dogs Red and Fred, their fleas Itch and Scratch, and their cattle Brawny Bull and Helen Heifer.

Chapter 3

OUTSMARTING SOURPUSS JONES

Cowboy Little and Cowboy Small woke up just as the first light of dawn peeked over the mountains rising behind Two Gulch Gap. Red and Fred were already awake with their ears perked up.

"I bet they hear something we can't," said Cowboy Small.

The boys fried the ham and biscuits Mama had packed. After breakfast, they rinsed the sleep from their eyes and washed their hands in the cool, clear waters of Cripple Creek. Then they stood up as tall, brave, and proud as two very little cowboys can be.

"Let's git a move on," said Cowboy Little.

Suddenly, Red and Fred began barking their meanest barks. Fred bared his teeth and growled deep down in his throat.

"Uh oh," said Cowboy Little. "Someone is coming up the trail."

As the lone cowboy came into sight, Cowboy Small whispered, "Uh oh. It's Sourpuss Jones on his sorry ol' mare. Grandpa says he's one of the meanest members of the Whiskey Still Gang—the one who does the most stealin' and fightin.'"

"Remember that time when Daddy caught him trying to steal a calf from the Circle R? Sourpuss fibbed and said he had found it wandering around and was bringing it back. But Daddy said he was headin' in the wrong direction," said Cowboy Little. "No way he meant to give it back."

"He gives me the shivers," said Cowboy Small.

"Me, too," said Cowboy Little.

Sourpuss Jones ambled up to the camp. With a tip of his beat-up black cowboy hat, he said all friendly-like, "Well, howdy boys. I saw smoke from your fire from a ways off. I thought you would have a cup of coffee and some breakfast for me."

"Sorry, but we don't have no breakfast, Mr. Sourpuss," Cowboy Small answered. "We got a little coffee left, if you want a sip. But we already 'et up all the ham and biscuits."

While Sourpuss slurped down the coffee, Cowboy Small and Cowboy Little saddled up their horses. They packed their saddlebags and rounded up the animals.

"How kin we git rid of him so we kin fetch the saddlebags?" whispered Cowboy Small. "We gotta head back to the Circle R pronto."

Sourpuss solved their problem. "I'm goin' down to the creek to git me some water," he said. "I'll be back di-rectly. I hope you're not in a big hurry to leave. I got a question fer you."

As soon as Sourpuss Jones was out of sight, Cowboy Little dashed into the cave and grabbed the saddlebags. He dragged them back to camp and threw them across Ned's back.

Cowboy Small jumped onto Ted and grabbed the reins dangling from Sourpuss's ol' mare. Then the cowboys and their animal friends took off down the trail, just as Sourpuss came back to the campsite.

"Boys, don't leave me way out here without my horse!" he yelled. "I'm old and I'm lame. I can't walk all the way back to town."

When they didn't stop, he yelled louder. "'Jist you wait! You brats are gonna be real sorry you messed with me!"

A mile or so down Cripple Creek Trail, Cowboy Small's conscience nagged at him. "Even though he's mean and scary, I can't leave Sourpuss all alone at Two Gulch Gap without a horse," he said. "I'm goin' to turn this ol' mare loose. She'll find her way back to him."

Three hours later, Cowboy Little and Cowboy Small, their horses Ned and Ted, their dogs Red and Fred, their fleas Itch and Scratch, and their cattle Brawny Bull and Helen Heifer arrived back at the Circle R ranch house. The little cowboys slid off their saddles. They grabbed the mysterious saddlebags and ran inside yelling, "Mama, Daddy, Grandpa Jake, Grandma Hettie, come quick!"

When no one answered, they yelled even louder.

Finally, Grandpa Jake moseyed out of his bedroom. "How come you two are making so much racket?" he griped. "There ain't nobody home but me. You woke me from my nap."

"You kin nap later," said Cowboy Little. "Wait 'til you see the mysterious treasures we found."

As the boys emptied the saddlebags, Grandpa Jake's eyes got big as an owl's behind his wire-rimmed glasses. He picked up each article. "Fellas, I'm mighty impressed. Mighty impressed. I think one of the things y'all found is the famous Old Lost Map. There's been a rumor for more'n fifty years that it points the way to a cave filled with gold coins. I never believed the stories about the map were for real, but you sure enough might have found it."

The minute Mama, Daddy, and Grandma Hettie came back to the ranch house, the little cowboys pounced on them.

"Come quick, we have something special to show you," said Cowboy Little. He grabbed Grandma Hettie's hand and pulled her toward the table.

"Last night at Two Gulch Gap, we found some real old saddlebags filled with gold coins and a treasure map," said Cowboy Small.

"And this morning, Sourpuss Jones came ridin' up to the campsite," said Cowboy Little.

"Uh oh," said Grandpa Jake. "Ol' Sourpuss always means trouble."

Grandma Hettie's eyes were glued to the pile of gold coins. "I ain't never seen so much gold in all my life," she said.

"Me neither," said Mama. She held a coin up to the sunlight. "Jist lookee how it shines."

Cowboy Big and Cowboy Tall came through the door. "How come everybody's sittin' round the table?" said Cowboy Big. "It ain't suppertime yet."

"Come see," said the little boys at the same time. "Lookee what we found."

While Grandpa Jake studied the map, Daddy picked up the medical dictionary. "This here is the strangest thing of all," he said. "Why would a cowboy be totin' a medical dictionary? And what about these letters here? What do you make of all this strange stuff, Grandpa Jake?"

"Let's not git ahead of ourselves. We need to have a good look-see before we start guessing the answers," said Grandpa Jake. He slowly unfolded the letters and began reading them. "Looks like they were writ by some lady named Nell to her husband who was prospecting for gold. They're addressed to Joe in care of Shep's Trading Post. I reckon he means back in the day when Pegleg Shep's great-granddaddy owned the tradin' post," said Grandpa Jake. "But the letters don't say nothin' that will help us fig'er things out."

"Wait a minute," said Daddy as he picked one up. "There's some other writin' on the back from Joe to Nell. This 'un reads:

> "'Dearest Nell, please tell my children I think of them often and miss them plenty. I met up with a Hopi Indian chief. He's done showed me some stuff he got from his granddaddy that was left behind by some Spanish soldiers. He says they came to these here parts long, long ago. He had some shields and a couple of fancy swords. There was a map made by somebody else that might lead to buried Spanish gold. I'm headin' out tomorrow to look fer it. If I find the gold, we'll surely be rich. With great affection, I remain your husband, Joe.'"

When Daddy finished reading the letter out loud, Grandpa Jake said, "Y'all gather round and I'll tell you a story. A long,

long time ago, there was an old prospector named Joe. I reckon it's the same Joe in the letters. He worked a gold mine up in the mountains. He's said to have found some saddlebags filled with gold coins. He also had a map leading to the place where he thought many more were hidden. Poor Joe died long ago under very strange circumstances. Prob'ly murdered. As far as I recollect, no one has ever before laid eyes on the saddlebags, the gold coins, or the map."

As the grown-ups talked, Cowboy Little and Cowboy Small gave each other a bear hug. They were real proud of themselves.

"Far as I can tell, there's no way to find the rightful owners," said Daddy. "You say Joe died a long, long time ago, and there's not a clue about where Nell and his children lived? One thing I know for sure—there's no way the saddlebags belong to the Whiskey Still Gang, unless they stole 'em."

"Maybe if we fig'er out how to read the map, that will give us a clue to the owners," said Grandpa Jake. "I think the gold circle in the corner marks the hidin' place, but I ain't sure."

Suddenly, Red and Fred growled and Ned and Ted whinnied. Even Brawny Bull and Helen Heifer pawed the ground and made a racket. Then came the sound of thundering hooves. Everyone froze.

"I bet that's Sourpuss Jones and his sorry bunch of bandits come looking for the saddlebags," said Daddy. "He might've been the one who stole 'em and left 'em at Two Gulch Gap. Cowboy Little, run down to the bunkhouse and tell the cowhands to git up here and be ready for a little action."

Cowboy Little ran as fast as his short legs could carry him

and came back with eight cowhands. They lined up on the porch next to Cowboy Big, Cowboy Tall, Grandpa Jake, and Daddy, and cocked their rifles. Mama, Grandma Hettie, Cowboy Little, and Cowboy Small hid behind the parlor curtains to listen.

Sure enough, it was the Whiskey Still Gang. The ugliest, meanest bunch of cowboys the boys had ever seen galloped up to the house and lined up facing the porch. Every one of them wore a black cowboy hat.

"We come for the saddlebags your young'uns stole from us!" Sourpuss Jones yelled.

Grandpa Jake stepped to the edge of the wide porch that encircled the ranch house. "Sourpuss, you and your gang go on about your business. This here is private property, and you're not welcome."

Their leader, Thurman Roundtree, who had a big jagged scar on his face, rode his horse right up to the porch steps. "Lookee here," he said. "We found those saddlebags fair and square, but somehow left 'em behind. Sourpuss Jones thought I had 'em, and I thought he had 'em. So, they got left at Two Gulch Gap, where your brats found them. They belong to us."

Grandpa Jake stood real tall and cocked his gun. "I told you, git off my property."

Hearing those words, the men of Circle R Ranch raised their guns.

The Whiskey Still Gang looked around and likely figured out that they were outgunned. "This here is a promise," Thurman Roundtree shouted. "We'll be back!" They turned their horses around and thundered down the road.

"I'm gonna post lookouts in case they come back tonight," said Daddy, "but first we need to hide everything, 'specially the coins."

"How about putting the coins in the well?" asked Cowboy Little.

"That's the first place they'd look," said Cowboy Small.

"How 'bout under the mattresses?"

"That's the second place they'd look," said Grandpa Jake.

"What about in the Johnny pot in the bedroom?" Cowboy Tall suggested.

"Gross," said Cowboy Little.

"Let's hide 'em in my butter churn," said Grandma Hettie. "There's one sittin' near the fireplace warmin' the milk 'til it turns into buttermilk. Nobody would ever look there."

Daddy nodded and dropped all the coins into the butter churn. "What about the medical book and the moccasins?" he asked.

"Let's put 'em behind the bookcase in the parlor," said Cowboy Small. "Those sorry cowboys can't read. They'd never look there."

"That's a dandy idea," said Mama.

As soon as everything was tucked out of sight, Cowboy Little asked Daddy, "How kin we find out what the coins are worth?"

"Well," said Daddy, "the best man for that is Earl Cash in the assayer's office in Johnsonville. If anyone'll know what they're worth, it's him."

"Kin we ride into town tomorrow to ask him? Pu-lease," begged Cowboy Small.

"Only if Cowboy Big and Cowboy Tall go with you," Daddy said. "The Whiskey Still Gang might take off after you, and you fellas wouldn't be no match for that bunch of thieves."

The next morning the four brothers took two of the gold coins to the assayer's office in Johnsonville, where prospectors brought their gold ore to be weighed. It was smack dab across the street from the sheriff's office so he and his deputies could keep an eye out for trouble.

"Howdy, Mr. Cash," said Cowboy Tall as they walked through the door. "We ran across some gold coins. Think you kin tell us what they're worth?"

"I'll sure give it my best shot," he said. He picked up his magnifying glass to read the markings. "Wherever did you boys find these? These here gold coins were brought to these parts by Spanish soldiers long, long ago. I hear tell they traded them with the trappers," he said. "They're worth a heap of money today."

Cowboy Big and Cowboy Tall let out a whoop while Cowboy Little and Cowboy Small danced a jig.

"Do you want to sell 'em? I'll offer you a fair price," the assayer said.

"Not right now," said Cowboy Tall. "Maybe Grandpa Jake will come talk to you next week."

As the four cowboys left, Mr. Cash warned, "Don't tell no one what you found, else you'll have a lot of greedy cowboys coming after 'em."

Cowboy Big said, "Yes, sir. We're much obliged for the advice."

By the time they got back to the Circle R, Cowboy Little and Cowboy Small were plumb tuckered out. They could barely stay awake during dinner. They even went to bed without being told. With Red and Fred curled up on the floor, they dreamed about their exciting adventure at Two Gulch Gap with their horses Ned and Ted, their dogs Red and Fred, their fleas Itch and Scratch, and their cattle Brawny Bull and Helen Heifer.

Chapter 4

ASKED AND ANSWERED

Everyone was up long before sunrise the next morning. They all worried that the Whiskey Still Gang would come back to raid the house looking for the gold coins.

"We need to put all them in the strong box at the bank, except for two that we can put back in the butter churn," said Daddy. "We might run across somebody in these parts who can fig'er out where they come from.

"But I had another idea last night. I writ a letter to Governor Ordway, the territorial governor, and put one of the coins into the envelope and asked him to tell us what he knows. I bet my last dollar he'll answer. We kin mail it in town."

"Please, kin we go, too?" begged Cowboy Little. "We're the ones who found the gold coins."

"Pu-lease!" said Cowboy Small. "Pu-lease!"

Daddy thought for a minute. "Okay, boys. It's only right for you to have a hand in their safe keepin'. But y'all be sure and bring your rifles jist in case we run into trouble."

Riding in the wagon on the way to Johnsonville, Cowboy

Little and Cowboy Small kept a sharp lookout for the Whiskey Still Gang. Nary a one was in sight.

"I'm sure glad we didn't run into trouble on the way," said Daddy. "Let's git the gold coins to the bank pronto and mail the letter to the governor."

With their missions complete, they headed out the post-office door. Cowboy Little stopped dead in his tracks. "Uh oh. Lookee there. Sourpuss Jones is leanin' up ag'in our wagon across the street."

Daddy hurried toward Sourpuss. "That there ain't your wagon," he yelled. "It belongs to me and it's leavin' shortly. You best be on your way."

Sourpuss stomped up to Daddy right close. "I know you done put my gold coins in the bank," he said. "And I'm gonna git what's rightfully mine."

"Well, Sourpuss, I'm gonna give you some advice. You done already spent time in the pokey, and if you mess with things that ain't yours, you're gonna spend more."

"You don't scare me, Rancher Randall," said Sourpuss. "One way or t'other, I'm gonna git my gold back." He gave the boys a mean look. Then he walked across the street and into the saloon.

Cowboy Little and Cowboy Small pretended to be brave, but their hearts were beating a fast tune inside their chests.

"Come on, boys," said Daddy. "Let's us git a move on."

Before they left Johnsonville, Daddy stopped in at the sheriff's office. "Sheriff Posey," said Daddy, "I'm skeered that the Whiskey Still Gang may try and rob the bank. We done put some things in the strong box they think belong to them. They don't. It's historical stuff. We've sent a sample to Governor Ordway to find out what it really is. But you need to keep an eye out. Sourpuss Jones is tryin' to fig'er out the best way for the Whiskey Still Gang to git their hands on our stuff."

"I appreciate the warning, Rancher Randall, but we ain't had a successful bank robbery in this town since I got elected sheriff. I'm gonna make sure it don't happen anytime soon."

"Thank you, Sheriff Posey. We're much obliged. Say hi to the missus for me."

The boys and Daddy got back on the wagon and headed toward the ranch. Sourpuss was nowhere in sight.

***

For the boys, the following weeks in school seemed to take forever. They couldn't wait for the letter from the governor to arrive.

Grandpa Jake and Daddy were as eager as the little cowboys. As they sat near the fireplace puffing on their corncob pipes one night, Grandpa said, "Do you remember Ranger John Reid?"

"I reckon I do, but we ain't seen him in these parts for many a year."

"He's done retired from being a ranger, but we were good friends in the old days," said Grandpa Jake. "He rode all over these parts, from the Texas border to Oklahoma, keepin' the peace. He made friends with a lot of the Indian tribes and might be able to crack the secret of the map."

"Let's write him a letter and ask him to visit for a spell," Daddy suggested. "As I recall, he could spin great yarns about the Old West. He even told stories way back to the time when Spanish soldiers roamed these parts. Maybe the last of them hid the saddlebags somewhere."

The next day, Grandpa Jake hitched up the wagon to go into town to pick up some more supplies from the general store. The boys wanted to see if Daddy had gotten an answer from the governor, so they begged to come along.

"If Daddy says it's okey dokey, then it's okey dokey with me," said Grandpa. "I'll be glad for the company. And you boys kin help me load up the supplies."

On the long ride into town in the creaky buckboard, Cowboy Little and Cowboy Small sang cowboy songs and told Grandpa Jake silly jokes. While he shopped for supplies, the boys darted into the post office inside the bank. They wanted to mail the letter to Ranger John Reid, and they also wanted to see if Daddy had gotten an answer from Governor Ordway.

Cowboy Small handed the letter addressed to Ranger Reid to the old man behind the counter. "Do you have any mail for our daddy, Rancher Randall?" he asked.

The boys held their breath.

"Well, let's see," the old man said. He thumbed through a pile of mail. "I'll be a monkey's uncle. Here's one addressed to Rancher Randall at the Circle R. Looks like it's from the governor of the territory. It could be real important. Take care you don't lose it."

"We promise," said Cowboy Little and Cowboy Small. They raced out of the post office to find Grandpa Jake.

"Grandpa, Grandpa," Cowboy Little said. "Guess what! Daddy got an answer from Governor Ordway. We can't wait 'til we git home to hear what it says. Read it to us now, pu-lease!"

Grandpa looked at their excited faces. "Well, you know it's ag'in the law to open a letter addressed to someone else." Then he winked and opened the envelope. *"Dear Rancher Randall,"* Grandpa whispered so no one else could hear. *"I received your letter along with the gold coin. We took it to the state assayer, who said the coin was made in Spain. Each one of this size is worth about two hundred dollars."*

The boys' mouths dropped open. "We counted more'n fifty gold coins! No wonder the Whiskey Still Gang wants them back."

Grandpa whispered, "That's ten thousand dollars, a gen-u-ine fortune. I ain't never seen that much money in my whole life. But, if we want to learn more about the strange things you boys found, we have to solve the mystery of the map."

"The governor said it came from Spain? Where's that?" asked Cowboy Small. "We ain't never heared tell of it."

"It's way far away across a big ocean," Grandpa said. "It's been told that a bunch of explorers from Spain came to these here parts long, long ago. They likely used the coins to trade with trappers."

When they got back to the ranch, Daddy read the letter out loud to Mama and Grandma Hettie. "Grandpa Jake, that was one swell idea of yours to write to Ranger Reid to help us fig'er it all out. I sure hope he comes to visit for a spell," said Daddy.

That night when they went to bed, the little cowboys

dreamed about getting the letter from the governor and finding more treasure with their daddy and grandpa, their horses Ned and Ted, their dogs Red and Fred, their fleas Itch and Scratch, and their cattle Brawny Bull and Helen Heifer.

Chapter 5

RANGER REID TO THE RESCUE

Over the next few weeks, the little cowboys could hardly think about anything but Ranger Reid. "How long before he answers?" they asked Grandpa Jake.

"All we can do is wait. Maybe Ranger Reid will write back. Or, maybe he'll jist show up one day."

Things were normal at the Circle R Ranch for a couple of weeks. Everyone was busy rounding up the cattle for branding, even Cowboy Little and Cowboy Small, who had help from their dogs Red and Fred.

One evening at suppertime, they heard somebody holler, "Howdy! Howdy in the house. Anyone inside?"

The little cowboys ran to the window. There in the front yard was an old cowboy dressed all in black, except for his white hat. He was riding a beautiful white horse. "Come quick, Grandpa Jake!" Cowboy Little called. "I reckon this is Ranger Reid."

Grandpa hurried out the door. "Welcome, welcome, Ranger Reid. It's good to see you and Silver after all these years. These boys have pestered me to death wonderin' when we'd hear from you."

"That's a mighty interesting letter you sent me, Jake. It really got my curiosity goin'," said Ranger Reid. "I thought I'd take you up on your invite to visit for a spell. Maybe I kin help you fig'er out what the boys found."

Mama fixed Ranger Reid a big plate of steak and potatoes and poured him some piping-hot coffee. After he finished, he said, "Ma'am, that's the best meal I've had in many a moon. I'm mighty obliged for your hospitality."

The men settled into rocking chairs and lit up their corncob pipes.

Daddy said, "Cowboy Little and Cowboy Small, tell Ranger Reid how you found the saddlebags."

"I want to tell him," said Cowboy Little.

"No, me," said Cowboy Small. "Everyone knows I'm the best storyteller."

Cowboy Little pouted, then plopped down on the hearth.

"We went camping up at Two Gulch Gap near the North 40," said Cowboy Small. "Someone left the campsite a mess. I went to catch us a trout for supper while Cowboy Little went lookin' for firewood. That's when he found the saddlebags hidden between two big rocks."

Ranger Reid looked surprised. "No self-respecting cowboy leaves his saddlebags behind. What did you fellas do when you found 'em?"

"Same as anybody, I reckon," said Cowboy Little. "We opened them up pronto. We found all sorts of interestin' things. There was even a pouch full of gold coins. Before we went to sleep, we hid the saddlebags in the bat cave nearby."

Cowboy Small butted in, "Sourpuss Jones rode up the next morning and asked us if we had any food. But I think he was really lookin' for the saddlebags. While he was down at the creek, Cowboy Little fetched 'em from the cave where we hid 'em. I grabbed the reins of Sourpuss's horse so he couldn't foller us, then we took off for the Circle R. After a while, I felt bad about leaving Sourpuss alone way up there, so I let his mare loose. I knew she'd find her way back to him."

"Since we had a big head start, we got home without any trouble. We showed Grandpa Jake, Grandma Hettie, Daddy, Mama, and Cowboy Big and Cowboy Tall all the mysterious things. Then we hid them real good," said Cowboy Little.

"Later, the Whiskey Still Gang came riding right up to the porch," said Grandpa Jake. "They wanted the saddlebags. I fibbed and said we didn't have 'em. I knew they didn't rightly belong to that bunch of bandits, especially not the medical dictionary. When we cocked our rifles, they high-tailed it off the Circle R. But sometimes I see 'em hanging around outside the gate. I guess they're hopin' we'll lead 'em to the gold coins."

Ranger Reid looked at the little boys. "If the Whiskey Still Gang wants to git their hands on it, you two must have found something mighty special," he said. "Let's take a look-see at what all you found."

Cowboy Little scurried around to fetch the treasures from their hiding places. Cowboy Small stuck his hand into the butter churn to pull out the two gold coins from the bottom. They were so slimy, he had to rinse them in Mama's washtub.

"How come I git all the messy jobs?" he muttered.

"Because I'm way older than you. You have to do what I say," said Cowboy Little.

Cowboy Small wanted to wrestle his brother to the ground, but Ranger Reid was visiting. Instead, he gave Cowboy Little a fierce look and whispered, "I'll git you later."

Ranger Reid fingered the coins. "The governor told you they come by way of Spanish soldiers?" he asked. "I reckon he's dead right. They might of hid the saddlebags so they could fetch 'em later. Guess that time never came," he said. "Where are the coins now?"

"Except for these two, they're safe in the Johnsonville Bank's strong box," replied Daddy.

Ranger Reid spread out the map. Without saying a word, he turned it this way and that. Cowboy Little and Cowboy Small were about to burst with curiosity.

Finally, he grinned. "I think I know the place marked by the sign of the yellow circle. Looks like it's near Humphrey's Peak. It's the only range in these here parts with three peaks like on the map. I've also made the acquaintance of an old Hopi Indian by the name of Chief Tocho. His great-great-granddaddy was chief when the Spaniards came through these parts. Stories are passed down from generation to generation in Indian tribes. If he heard the tales, he'll remember. I reckon we ought to pay him a visit."

Cowboy Little and Cowboy Small jumped up and down. "You'll take us with you, won't you?" asked Cowboy Little. "We ain't never seen Indians up real close."

Ranger Reid threw back his head and laughed. "How could

I leave the two best treasure hunters behind? It's a day's ride to the Hopi village where the map will make more sense. But for now, hide it to keep it safe."

Chapter 6

COWBOYS AND INDIANS

Cowboy Little, Cowboy Small, and Ranger Reid began making plans to leave the next day.

"Whoa," said Daddy. "We'll need more than jist two boys and a retired ranger with us in case the Whiskey Still Gang makes trouble. I reckon Grandpa Jake and our best cowhands, Cowboy Slim and Cowboy José, should go along."

Early the next morning, the group packed up their supplies and headed out. About the time the boys' tummies started rumbling, they stopped near a babbling brook to water the animals and eat some vittles.

Soon, Ranger Reid said, "Time to saddle back up, fellas. We've still got a long ride ahead."

They came into a beautiful little valley just before sunset. "The Hopi Indians live over yonder in those adobe houses on the side of the hill," he said.

"I thought Indians lived in teepees," said Cowboy Small.

"Tribes that do a lot of huntin' foller the herds and move their teepees," said Ranger Reid. "But the Hopis are farmers and make silver jewelry and pottery. They stay in one place and build houses out of mud and straw on the side of the mountains."

The Circle R cowboys rode slowly toward the village. All of a sudden, six Indian braves on painted ponies came charging toward them. The braves whooped and shook their spears.

"They don't look happy to see white men on their land," whispered Cowboy Little. "I'm skeered."

"Not me!" Cowboy Small whispered back. He puffed out his chest, tryin' to look fierce.

Ranger Reid raised his right hand with the palm forward to show they had come in peace. He used sign language to talk to the braves, the same way he did when he was keeping peace in the territory.

One brave galloped toward the village. The rest circled the group.

"What did you say to them?" whispered Grandpa.

"I told 'em, 'I'm John Reid, a friend of Chief Tochos. I come in peace with my friends. Will you take us to your chief?'"

When the brave came back, he signed to Ranger Reid to follow him.

"Jist be calm and don't spook the rest of the braves," Ranger Reid told the group. "I'll be back di-rectly."

After a time, Ranger Reid and the brave came galloping back.

"Okay, fellas, we're in good shape. Jist foller me. We're gonna sit around the council fire with the chief and powwow fer a bit."

When they rode into the village, Ranger Reid made the peace sign. He pulled some coffee and tobacco from his saddlebags and handed them to the chief. "We thank you for welcoming us onto your reservation," he said in sign language. "I brought some tobacco and coffee for you. I know you can't always git them way out here."

Before long, he and Chief Tocho were signing back and forth.

Cowboy Little and Cowboy Small watched in awe. "Let's ask Ranger Reid to teach us sign language," whispered Cowboy Small. "We could trick all our school friends. It'll drive them crazy wantin' to know what we're saying."

Ranger Reid had told them the Hopis were a peaceful tribe known for getting along with the white men who loved the West, too. But the boys were surprised to be invited to share a meal. After they ate their fill, the men sat cross-legged in a circle and passed a peace pipe around.

The little cowboys tried to make out what they were saying, but grew tired. About then, they spotted four little Indian braves staring at them. Cowboy Little said, "Let's show them the jumpin' flea trick."

"Yeah," said Cowboy Small. "That's a great idea."

Cowboy Small held up his hand in peace like Ranger Reid.

"Follow me," said one in English. "My name is Hototo. Chief Tocho is my daddy. Do you want to play with us?"

The boys were surprised the Indians spoke English. "Where did you learn to speak our language?" Cowboy Little asked.

"At the mission school," Hototo explained.

"Do y'all want to see the jumpin' flea contest?" asked Cowboy Little. The Hopi boys nodded. Cowboy Little and Cowboy Small pulled their white kerchiefs out of their pockets and laid them on the ground. They placed the matchboxes so they faced one another, and then opened them slowly. As soon as the little Indian braves saw the fleas, they jumped back.

"Uh oh," said Hototo. "Will they bite us?"

"Nah," said Cowboy Little. "These here are our pet fleas, Itch and Scratch. They never bite anyone unless we tell them to. Come in closer so you kin see.

"Here's how the contest works. The flea that jumps the highest gits a tiny piece of meat for dinner. We've done this lot-sa times. Itch and Scratch know what to do. Y'all help us decide which one wins."

The fleas flitted out of their boxes and lit on the white ker-chiefs. Cowboy Little clapped his hands, and Itch and Scratch jumped. The Indians thought it was the funniest thing they'd ever seen. Then they clapped again and again. Before long, Itch was jumping a foot higher off the white scarf than Scratch. Act-ing like a sore loser, Scratch flitted back into his box and sulked. They all declared Itch the winner, and Cowboy Small put a tiny piece of meat in his box.

After a while, the boys drifted back toward the campfire to watch Ranger Reid and Chief Tocho signing.

When the moon settled behind a cloud and the stars twin-kled above, Grandpa thanked Chief Tocho. Ranger Reid translat-ed his words. "We need to set up camp and get our boys settled down for the night," he said. "But we'd be pleased to come back tomorrow. There's something we want to ask your council."

The Circle R cowboys chose a spot near the creek and built a campfire. Everyone spread out their bedrolls under the stars and turned in for the night. But after their successful meet-up with the Indians, Grandpa Jake was feeling playful. As everyone was crawling into their bedrolls, he took out a bullet and wedged it into a split green branch with the pointed end up. Ranger Reid was the only one watching him, and he was trying real hard to keep from laughing.

When that bullet heated up and exploded, it made a *BANG!* so loud, it was likely heard way back at the Indian reservation. It sounded just like a gunshot.

Cowboy Little, Cowboy Small, and everyone else at the campsite jumped up, grabbed their rifles, and looked all around to see where the shot might'a come from. The boys were scared. The horses were neighing. The dogs were barking, and the cattle were snorting and pawing the ground.

Grandpa Jake and Ranger Reid couldn't keep quiet any longer. They burst out laughing, so hard that tears rolled down their cheeks.

"I was jist funning you," Grandpa Jake said. "I thought we needed to liven up the camp a bit."

Daddy gave him a mean look. "You're too old for this foolishness, Grandpa Jake. Git on off to bed. You, too, boys."

After all the ruckus, Cowboy Little and Cowboy Small had a hard time getting to sleep. But in a while, they drifted off with their dogs Red and Fred at their sides, content that their horses Ned and Ted, their fleas Itch and Scratch, and their cattle Brawny Bull and Helen Heifer were nearby. They dreamed of sitting in the circle with their new Indian friends, using sign language instead of English.

Chapter 7

CHIEF TOCHO POINTS THE WAY

The next morning, the boys woke up to the smell of sizzling bacon, fried ham, and coffee. Ranger Reid said, "Grab some vittles, fellas, then let's go back to the Hopi village. Maybe Chief Tocho kin help us fig'er out the map. I'll ask if he's ever seen any caves on Humphrey's Peak."

Cowboy Little, Cowboy Small, Grandpa Jake, Daddy, and Ranger Reid rode back to the Hopi village while the cowhands looked after the animals.

"Lookee," whispered Cowboy Little, "Chief Tocho is wearing moccasins like the ones we found in the saddlebags."

Using sign language, the chief thanked Ranger Reid for the coffee and tobacco, and Ranger Reid praised the beautiful beadwork on his moccasins.

"The golden eagle in flight has been the symbol of the Hopi tribal chiefs for many generations," the chief signed.

Before Ranger Reid had a chance to sign back, Chief Tocho laughed out loud. In English he said, "Why don't we jist stop signing and talk in your language?"

Ranger Reid slapped his knee and guffawed. "You got me," he said. "I reckon you went to the mission school to learn English."

"Most of our young ones, too," said the chief proudly.

"Chief, here's my question," said Ranger Reid. "Did your ancestors tell you any stories about the time when people from a faraway land tried to invade the West?"

The chief nodded. "Many stories were passed down by my great-great-grandfather to my father. The Hopis farmed on this land for centuries and lived in peace with tribes around us. But then the soldiers from Spain came to these parts and everything changed. They took away our land and made us slaves. But, during my great-great-grandfather's time as chief, the Hopis joined other tribes to drive the Spanish devils away. We took our land back. Today, our reservation reaches even farther than the eye kin see."

"Did the braves ever hide in caves up in the mountains?" Ranger Reid asked.

Chief Tocho nodded. "There's a great cave on the peak closest to the rising sun that we've known about for many, many years," he said. "When we were fighting the Spanish, our braves hid there and planned an attack. Later, deer and turkey got scarce, and we had to go farther to find meat. If we were near the mountains, we stayed in the same cave. It's a three-day ride from here."

Daddy popped in, "Can you tell us more about that cave? Cowboy Little and Cowboy Small want to explore."

"Well, there's not much there now. When I was a young

brave, I saw some old buffalo skins deep inside. But the last time I was there, a pile of rocks covered everything up. I didn't fig'er it was worth digging them out."

Ranger Reid and Daddy stood up, and the boys scrambled to their feet. "We thank you for your help," said Ranger Reid. "But I want to give you a warning. If a group of sorry-looking cowboys wearing black hats rides up here, be on your guard. The leader has a jagged scar on his cheek. Another cowboy has a sour look on his face. They're up to no good."

"Thank you for the warning," said Chief Tocho. "Be well and go in peace. You are always welcome on the reservation."

The chief shook hands with everyone, even Cowboy Little and Cowboy Small. The boys couldn't stop smiling. Then the Circle R crew saddled up and headed toward the Humphrey's Peak.

Suddenly, Daddy reined in his horse. "Hold up, boys," he said. "We need to think on this. We suspect the saddlebags came from that cave on Humphrey's Peak. But, based on what the chief said, it's a three-day ride. Add that on to the day it took to git to the Hopi village. That makes near ten days back and forth—maybe more if we explore. Right now, we need to head back to the Circle R Ranch. School will be out in two weeks' time."

"Aw, Daddy. We want to go now," whined Cowboy Small.

"Yeah," said Cowboy Little, stamping his foot. "Right now!"

Daddy gave them the look he used when they were in big trouble. The boys kept quiet.

"I agree," said Ranger Reid. "We're not prepared for such a

long trip right now. In a few weeks we kin stock up on vittles. We'll take a pack mule to carry the food and tents."

Cowboy Little and Cowboy Small pouted. They slowly turned Ned and Ted around. They whistled to their dogs Red and Fred, their fleas Itch and Scratch, and their cattle Brawny Bull and Helen Heifer. Grumbling, they followed the grown-ups back to the Circle R.

Mama breathed a sigh of relief when she saw them. "I was skeered the Whiskey Still Gang would foller y'all and make trouble," she said.

"Nah," said Daddy. "We were fine. We even met the Hopi chief."

"You should have seen the Indian village, Mama," said Cowboy Small. "They live in baked-mud houses on the side of the mountain. We sat around their campfire with the braves and a real Indian chief. The chief even wore moccasins like the ones we found in the saddlebags."

"And he could speak English," said Cowboy Little. "He told us about some caves far, far away on Humphrey's Peak. It has three peaks and looks like the ones on the treasure map. When school is out, we're goin' on a real long adventure with Ranger Reid and Daddy."

"With the help of the Hopis, we made good progress in figuring out the mysterious map," Daddy said. "We couldn't have done it without Ranger Reid. He knows where the Hopis live, and can even talk to them in sign language."

As the boys sat around the warm fireplace listening to the family talk, their eyes grew heavy.

"Time for bed," said Mama. "Tomorrow is a school day." She shooed them off to their bunks, but their heads were so filled with thoughts about the next great adventure with Daddy and Ranger Reid that they didn't even complain.

Chapter 8

SEARCH FOR THE HIDDEN TREASURE

Cowboy Little and Cowboy Small had a hard time paying attention in school those last two weeks. All they could think about was their big adventure with Ranger Reid.

Finally, school was out for the summer. The teacher dismissed the classes and everyone whooped and hollered. She had a wide grin on her face, too.

On the horseback ride home, Cowboy Little asked, "When we get to Humphrey's Peak, how will we know it's the right cave?"

"Maybe there will be clues, like lots of arrowheads," said Cowboy Small. "Ranger Reid will know."

The next morning, the boys were up before sunrise so they could do all their chores before leaving for Humphrey's Peak. Instead of going with them, Daddy asked Grandpa Jake to take his place. "Cowboy Big and Cowboy Tall and I need to stay on the Circle R to oversee planting the summer crop," he said. "Besides, if we all went along, there would be no one left to protect the womenfolk if the Whiskey Still Gang showed up."

As they were loading the big tent and the saddlebags filled with vittles onto the pack mule, Mama said, "Don't forget salt and a sack of flour for biscuits."

"And two slabs of bacon and lots of beans," said Ranger Reid.

"Be sure to take extra ammunition," said Daddy. "You might run into wild critters or the Whiskey Still Gang."

At the last minute, Mama ran out with a medicine kit. "You can't never tell when someone might git hurt," she said.

Everyone wrapped their bedrolls in slickers to keep them dry and loaded them on their horses. And while the menfolk gulped a last cup of coffee, Mama made the boys finish their milk.

"I sure do thank you for your hospitality, Miz Randall," said Ranger Reid. "I declare you're the best cook in the territory."

Mama blushed, but the boys could tell she was pleased.

The group headed single file down Cripple Creek Trail. Cowboy Small led the way on Ted. Cowboy Little came next on Ned, followed by Grandpa Jake, Ranger Reid, Cowboy José, Cowboy Slim, and the pack mule. Red and Fred scampered in and out of the horses' legs, barking happy barks. Itch and Scratch were snug in their boxes in Cowboy Small's pocket, and Brawny Bull and Helen Heifer brought up the rear.

They stopped at Two Gulch Gap to eat some biscuits and ham, and to let the animals rest and drink cold, clear water from Cripple Creek. Then they continued on the trail toward Humphrey's Peak.

When they came to a fork in the road, Ranger Reid said,

"The right fork leads to the Hopi Indian village. The left fork leads in the di-rection of Humphrey's Peak. But you'd best let me lead the way. Sometimes the trail is easy to foller. Other times it fades into the brush."

At sunset, the sky glowed with streaks of orange, red, purple, and pink, as if it were on fire. "Now ain't that the purtiest thing you ever seen?" asked Grandpa Jake.

"I've seen a million, gillion sunsets," said Cowboy Small, "and they're never the same. I don't ever get tired of watching 'em."

"Me neither," said Cowboy Little. "Grandpa Jake, can we stop right here and wait 'til the sun settles behind the hills?"

"Sure 'nuff," said Grandpa Jake. "This here valley is a great spot for sunset watching."

Just before dark, they set up camp. Cowboy José built a campfire and cooked up some stew while Cowboy Slim played sweet notes on his mouth harp that echoed through the valley.

The boys grinned. "What could be funner than this?" said Cowboy Little.

"Finding the rest of the treasure," said Cowboy Small. For once, his brother didn't disagree.

When the fire began to die, Grandpa Jake told everyone it was time to turn in. The boys reckoned *he* was the one who was tired. They wanted to hear some more songs. But, with the cool night air, warm bedrolls, and their dogs curled up beside them, the little cowboys fell sound asleep. They dreamed about piles of gold coins and arrowheads waitin' to be found in the cave.

The next morning, they headed toward Humphrey's Peak,

stopping only once to eat some grub and rest and water the animals. Cowboy Little and Cowboy Small were so excited, they could hardly sit still in their saddles.

"Hold up," signaled Ranger Reid when they finally reached the base of the tallest peak. "I think this here is what we've been looking for. Let's leave Brawny Bull and Helen Heifer at the bottom and see how high we can git on the horses."

The higher they went, the harder the climb. When it got too steep, Ranger Reid signaled. "Let's be smart about this, boys. We need to go back down to a level spot and set up base camp. We'll tackle the mountain a'gin in full daylight."

"But I see an opening in the mountain that might be a cave," said Cowboy Little, pointing to the left.

"I see one, too," said Cowboy Small. He pointed to the right. "Maybe it's the cave Chief Tocho told us about."

Ranger Reid held firm. Grandpa Jake agreed. "Come on, boys. Tomorrow will come soon enough."

Grumbling, they followed behind. They dragged the heels of their boots in the dirt to slow themselves down.

"No more of that," said Grandpa Jake in a stern voice. He hardly ever scolded, so they knew they'd best do as they were told.

The group bedded down for another night on the trail. Since they were halfway up the mountain, the weather was chilly. With their warm bedrolls around them and Red and Fred at their sides, Cowboy Little and Cowboy Small fell fast asleep near the campfire.

The next morning after breakfast, Cowboy Small asked, "When do we git started, Ranger Reid?"

"Is right now soon enough? Let's leave our horses and start climbing. Cowboy Slim, I'm'a trustin' you to keep the horses safe. There's bears in these here woods, and they're sure to spook the horses. If they run off, it'll be a mighty long walk back to the Circle R."

"You kin count on me," said Cowboy Slim as he pulled out his rifle.

Ranger Reid, Grandpa Jake, Cowboy Little, Cowboy Small, and Cowboy José began the trek up the mountain. The going was pretty steep. Every now and again the boys helped Grandpa Jake. Cowboy Little pulled him in front and Cowboy Small pushed from behind. When they reached a wide ledge, they spied a cave they hadn't seen the day before.

"Kin we go in first, pu-lease, pu-lease, Ranger Reid?" the little cowboys asked.

"Well, boys, what are you waiting for?" said Ranger Reid. "Go see what you kin see."

The opening wasn't large enough to walk in side by side, so Cowboy Little went first. Cowboy Small was right on his heels. They were barely inside when a cloud of bats flew at them. "Let's git out of here!" Cowboy Small screeched.

"Right now!" yelled Cowboy Little.

They were so spooked, they almost pushed one another down in their haste to squeeze back through the opening. Cowboy Little and Cowboy Small were shaking like saplings in the breeze. But instead of soothing them, Ranger Reid and Grandpa Jake laughed and slapped their knees.

"Now you boys ain't afraid of a few bats, are you?" said

Ranger Reid. "See, bats don't want to be around humans any more than humans want to be around them. They won't bother you if you don't bother them. But, you sure enough want to stay away from one lying still on the ground or actin' funny. They can carry some bad sicknesses."

Just like Ranger Reid said, the bats all disappeared in a flurry of black wings and weird chirps. As soon as they were gone, he led the group into the cave.

"There's some smoke soot on the walls and ceiling," said Grandpa Jake. "I'm purty sure someone must'a built a fire in here. But this here cave ain't big enough to be Chief Tocho's great-great-grandfather's huntin' cave."

They sat down in a small clearing outside the cave to have some grub, but the little cowboys were too disappointed to eat much.

"Y'all drink some water now and eat your food," said Grandpa Jake. "We've jist started our search."

Chapter 9

THE REAL DEAL

After lunch, the group climbed even higher. "Lookee," said Ranger Reid. "This here is an old trail that must lead some-where." They followed behind him until they came to a cave with a wide opening. "This 'un is plenty big enough to be the cave Chief Tocho told us about," said Ranger Reid. "And lookee there at the broken arrow."

Farther inside, there was a large room where the walls and ceiling were black with smoke and there was a fire circle in the middle of the floor. "No doubt now that Indians spent many a season here once upon a time," Ranger Reid said, pointing to the fire circle.

Way in the back was a narrow opening. But when they fol-lowed the narrow tunnel around a bend, they lost all the light. "We're gonna have to make us some pine torches if we want to go any deeper," said Ranger Reid. "Let's head back outside where we kin catch some light 'til Cowboy José kin fetch some."

Grandpa Jake and Ranger Reid plopped down, leaned up against the outside of the cave, and dozed off. But Cowboy Little and Cowboy Small couldn't sit still. They darted in and out, searching for arrowheads and hoping the bats wouldn't return.

Finally, Cowboy José came back with enough pine torches for everyone that he had found on the floor of the forest farther down the mountain. Grandpa Jake lit them with the matches he used for his corncob pipe. They held the torches high and walked through a narrow passage that opened up into a huge cavern. It was big enough for the entire Whiskey Still Gang and all their horses.

Ranger Reid pointed to some faded drawings of antelopes on the walls. "That there is more proof that Indians were once here. Let's see if they left anything behind." They headed toward a pile of rocks in the back corner that was almost as tall as Ranger Reid. "This might be the rockslide Chief Tocho told us about," said Ranger Reid. "Let's move the rocks so we kin see what's behind."

They formed a line and passed rocks from one to the other. After a long while, they had a small opening.

"Boys," said Ranger Reid, "stick your heads in there to see what you kin see."

The boys disappeared around a bend but came out pretty quickly. "This here passage opens up to an even bigger cavern with lots of weird stuff in it," said Cowboy Little. "But we gotta clear out more rocks so y'all kin git through."

"Now hold up," said Ranger Reid. "We gotta git back down the mountain to base camp before dark, eat dinner, and git a good night's rest. We'll tackle this in the morning."

"No, no, no!" wailed Cowboy Little and Cowboy Small. "We want to stay and look for treasure."

Grandpa Jake pointed his finger at them, a sure sign he was about to fuss. "Enough," he said. "You listen to Ranger Reid. He said it's time to go, so git along."

Hanging their heads, they trudged back to the base camp. Cowboy Slim had the fire ready for dinner, and as soon as he saw them round the bend, he put the pork chops and beans in the frying pan.

For the first time, the boys had a hard time falling asleep. When they finally drifted off, their dreams were filled with visions of the treasures and arrowheads they hoped to find.

The next morning, Cowboy Little and Cowboy Small got up early with Cowboy José and Cowboy Slim. They tended the fire while the cowhands rustled up the vittles.

"Purty please hurry," said Cowboy Little. "We want to go back to the big cave."

Ranger Reid said, "Hold up, boys. I'm gonna find us some better pine knots that'll last us a while." Before they could complain, he hopped on Silver and disappeared into the woods. When he came back, he had some sturdy pine torches tied to his saddlebag.

Back up the mountain they climbed.

As the boys led the way to the narrow opening, they heard a low growl and a *hiss-sss*.

"Wha-what's that?" Cowboy Small gasped. He held his torch up as high as he could. Near the opening sat Mama Mountain Lion. She *hiss-sssed* again. Then she roared.

"Back up real slow, fellas," said Ranger Reid. "We sure don't want to spook her. Let's git outta here and fig'er out what to do."

They tiptoed out of the cave and took shelter behind a

rock. They were close enough to see the cave's opening, but far enough away not to alert Mama Mountain Lion.

"Let's jist cool our heels for a while," said Ranger Reid. "Maybe she'll leave."

Like Ranger Reid had told them, Mama Mountain Lion came out of the cave a little while later, but she must not have caught the scent of the humans. When she headed down the mountain, the boys stepped back inside. Three of the furriest little cubs they'd ever seen came running. They were playing and jumping around like pet kittens.

"Uh oh. We got us a bigger problem now," said Ranger Reid. "Mama Mountain Lion is sure to come back to feed her cubs. I got an idea. Let's build a small fire next to the mouth of the cave. It'll fool her into thinkin' her cubs are in danger. I betcha she'll rescue them lickety-split."

Once the fire was goin' real good, they backed off a distance. It was hard for the boys to hold still until Mama Mountain Lion returned. She sniffed the air and roared.

"She's tryin' to fig'er out a way to get her cubs out without them getting burned," whispered Ranger Reid. Suddenly, she leaped around the edge of the fire and into the cave. Seconds later, she trotted out with one of the cubs in her mouth. The other two followed close behind.

"This is a great sign, fellas," Ranger Reid whispered. "I bet she's gone off to find another lair. I reckon the cave is ready for some explorin.'"

"Is it safe?" asked Cowboy Small. "I sure don't wanna become dinner for the cubs."

Ranger Reid laughed. "No need to be skeered. She's more 'n likely gone for good."

The boys scurried behind Grandpa into the second opening in the cave. "This 'un is even bigger than the first," he said.

"What's that turrible smell?" asked Cowboy Little. He pointed to the hump in the center of the cavern. "I sure hope it's not a dead critter."

"The smelly stuff on top is rotten buffalo hides," said Grandpa Jake. "I reckon Chief Tocho's great-great-grandfather used this cave to store hides until the rock slide locked 'em in. Let's move 'em out of the way so we kin search better."

The old hides coughed up a big cloud of dust and crumbled when touched, but the Circle R cowboys managed to clear them away. Underneath was a big mound of rocks that looked like a grave.

"Uh oh," said Grandpa Jake. "Be keerful not to disturb the dead."

Working together, they moved the rocks out of the way. But instead of a skeleton, they uncovered a deerskin sack.

"Kin *we* open it?" asked Cowboy Little.

"Take care," said Ranger Reid. "No tellin' what's inside."

The boys reached in and pulled out handfuls of arrowheads. "Jumpin' Jehoshaphat," said Cowboy Small. "Lookee at all these. I've never seen so many arrowheads in my whole life."

"These here are some of the purtiest I've ever seen," said Grandpa Jake. He picked a few arrowheads up and turned them over. "I reckon they were made from obsidian rock. It's real hard, shiny, and black, the best kind for making huntin' arrows."

While the boys fingered the arrowheads, Cowboy Slim reached into the hole and pulled out three war hatchets. The boys each grabbed one and danced and pranced in a circle, whoopin' and hollerin' like Hopi braves.

"Come over here, boys," said Grandpa Jake. "I found something really special, 'cept I don't rightly know what it is." Laying at his feet was a strange metal dish. It was silver and looked like a backward vest.

"I ain't never seen anything like that, not even in picture books," said Cowboy Small.

"I think this here is the kind of breastplate that Spanish soldiers wore in the olden days," said Ranger Reid. "I seen a picture of one hangin' on the wall at the governor's office. Let's git a better look."

While the grown-ups admired the fancy breastplate, Cowboy Little and Cowboy Small reached into the hole again. This time, they tugged at another deerskin bag, but it wouldn't budge. It was so heavy, it took Ranger Reid and Cowboy Slim working together to get it out.

"It jingles like the bag of coins we found in the saddlebag," said Cowboy Little. "I betcha it's more treasure!"

The boys put their hands into the bag. Out came fistfuls of gold coins that spilled onto the dirt floor. There were many, many more than were in the bag of coins the boys had found at Two Gulch Gap.

The grown-ups were speechless. Cowboy Little and Cowboy Small let out war whoops. "We found the treasure, we found the treasure! We're rich, we're rich!" they sang over and over.

Ranger Reid grinned at Cowboy Little and Cowboy Small. "Boys, we'd 'a never discovered all this if you hadn't found the map and gold coins in that old saddlebag. It led us to a true treasure. This here is way more gold than all the miners put together ever dug out of these mountains."

"You're the real hero, Ranger Reid," said Grandpa Jake. "We'd 'a never been able to find this fortune without your know-how about the Hopis and this neck of the woods."

For a few minutes, everyone sat in awe. Finally, Ranger Reid said, "There's way more coins here than we kin tote back to the ranch. Let's take all we kin carry in our saddlebags, then put the rest and the arrowheads back where they came from. We need to pray that nobody finds 'em 'afore we git back—'specially not the Whiskey Still Gang."

"How 'bout we turn that there breastplate upside down and use it like a bowl to hold the coins?" said Cowboy Small.

"Good thinkin'," said Ranger Reid.

"Kin we take the bag of arrowheads?" Cowboy Little asked. "Pu-lease?"

"We don't have room for 'em. They'll have to wait 'til the next trip," said Ranger Reid.

"Then can we purty please carry a few home in our pockets?" asked Cowboy Small. He looked like he was about to cry.

Grandpa Jake and Ranger Reid laughed. "Why, sure. Take three or four each," said Ranger Reid.

Before he could change his mind, the boys each grabbed a fistful of arrowheads and stuffed them in their pockets.

Everyone helped put fistfuls of coins onto the breastplate.

Then they buried the rest of the coins, the bag of arrowheads, and two of the hatchets back in the hole. Ranger Reid took the third one and put it through his belt so he'd have a souvenir of their adventure.

"Now we need to pile the rocks back on top," he said.

When they were done, Grandpa Jake looked around. "It looks near the same as it did when we found it," he said. "I reckon it's high time we head on down the mountain. Cowboy Little and Cowboy Small, find some tree limbs and walk behind us. We need to wipe out our tracks so nobody kin tell we've been here."

It was tough going down the slippery, rocky mountainside. Cowboy Slim and Ranger Reid carried the heavy breastplate with the bag of coins between them. They stumbled once, and it nearly tipped over, but Grandpa Jake steadied it in the nick of time.

The boys brought up the rear. They didn't want to leave any footprints, especially not their own. Both were scared the Whiskey Still Gang might figure out that the boys from the Circle R did, for true, find the saddlebags.

When the weary cowboys got to their base camp, everyone was dog-tired, but they were excited about the rare discovery. They shared the good news with Cowboy José, who helped load the coins into the saddlebags. He and Cowboy Slim wrapped the heavy breastplate in a couple of slickers so the pack mule could tote it back to the Circle R Ranch.

"How come we brought that funny breastplate instead of the arrowheads?" grumbled Cowboy Little.

"We need the breastplate to prove the coins were left behind by Spanish soldiers," said Ranger Reid. "It also made a handy way to carry those heavy coins."

"Is the treasure really ours?" asked Cowboy Small.

"Your pa and I will fig'er that out," said Grandpa Jake. "That trip to Two Gulch Gap when you found the saddlebags is the best adventure you'll ever have." He turned to Cowboy José and Cowboy Slim. "Don't worry, boys. Y'all will be well taken care of. But you have to give us your solemn promise you won't breathe a word about all this."

"You kin count on us," said Cowboy Slim. "We been part of the Circle R for nigh onto ten years. We're family."

Instead of spending the night at Humphrey's Peak, Ranger Reid said they should head back to the Circle R while they still had daylight. "Maybe we'll only have to spend one more night on the trail, and we can git home in time to help your daddy and brothers plant the summer crop."

Ranger Reid, Grandpa Jake, Cowboy José, Cowboy Slim, Cowboy Little, Cowboy Small, their horses Ned and Ted, their dogs Red and Fred, their fleas Itch and Scratch, and their cattle Brawny Bull, Helen Heifer, and the pack mule headed toward the ranch. They stopped just before dark and made camp near the Indian village. The next morning at dawn, they rode hard to the Circle R.

Hearing the pounding of the horses' hooves, Mama and Daddy came out on the porch.

"Well, fellas, what'd you find?" asked Daddy.

"Tell 'em, boys," said Ranger Reid.

Cowboy Little and Cowboy Small talked over one another. "We found it! We found the place marked on the map by the yellow circle," they said. "There were a jillion, million gold coins and a funny breastplate. Ranger Reid said it belonged to a Spanish soldier a long time ago."

"There was a pile of the purtiest arrowheads we've ever seen, but Grandpa Jake wouldn't let us bring home but a couple," said Cowboy Small.

"He promised we'll git them on the next trip," said Cowboy Little.

"Well, I'll be," said Daddy. "I'm dumbstruck. I never dreamed you'd find any more treasure."

The weary group headed into the house and sat down around the dinner table. After a day in their saddles, they were starving, so Mama heated up a big pot of beef stew loaded with carrots and potatoes from her garden. After everyone had their fill, they hid the pile of gold coins in the butter churn along with the two they had kept. There were so many, they reached halfway to the top.

"What about the breastplate?" asked Grandpa Jake.

"I have an idea," said Mama. "How 'bout we hang it over the fireplace like a decoration? It's so old, folks will think it's been there forever and won't pay it any never mind."

As soon as the rest of the coins were tucked away, the little cowboys began yawning.

"Off to bed with you," said Daddy. "You've had enough excitement for a while."

Before they fell asleep, they whispered about their adventure and the treasure they helped find. "I have a secret to tell you," said Cowboy Little. "I put some extra arrowheads in my pocket for you and me."

Cowboy Small giggled and reached into his boots on the floor beside his bed. "I did, too," he said.

As they drifted off to sleep, Cowboy Little and Cowboy Small dreamed about the cave where they discovered more gold coins and arrowheads than they would ever see again.

Chapter 10

MORE TREASURE

After their discovery at Humphrey's Peak, Ranger Reid rode off to visit an old friend for a few days. When he returned, he announced that it was time to return to the cave.

The little cowboys hooped and hollered.

As usual, the boys got up extra early to do their chores while the grown-ups loaded supplies onto the horses and the pack mule. Before long, they were ready for the trip. Ranger Reid led the way. Grandpa Jake, Cowboy José, Cowboy Slim, Cowboy Little, Cowboy Small, their horses Ned and Ted, their dogs Red and Fred, their fleas Itch and Scratch, and their cattle Brawny Bull, Helen Heifer, and the pack mule followed behind. Since they all knew where they were going, the trip seemed a lot shorter.

They camped in the same clearing partway up Humphrey's Peak, then climbed the rest of the way to the cave. Ranger Reid pulled out his Colt .45 in case Mama Mountain Lion or a bad bandit was waiting for them.

Ranger Reid went in first and signaled the others to wait

outside. "It don't look like anyone's been here since we left," he said. "Foller me."

When they got to the pile of rocks, Grandpa Jake cleared them out and pulled out the doeskin bag of arrowheads. He set them on the floor and pointed. "Boys, these here little ones were used to hunt small game like rabbits and squirrels. The bigger ones were fer killin' deer and antelope or any enemies who attacked the village.

"I've been thinking," he said. "Since Chief Tocho told us how to find this here cave, I reckon he'd be mighty appreciative to have the arrowheads. It's a rare collection, and his tribesmen probably carved them decades ago. I bet they consider them sacred."

"That's a dandy idea," said Ranger Reid.

Cowboy Little and Cowboy Small fingered the arrowheads carefully. "There are so many here. Kin we have some more for our collection?" Cowboy Little pleaded.

Ranger Reid could see hope shining in the boy's eyes. "Sure thing," he said gently. "Pick out a few from each size as souvenirs of this amazing adventure. But the rest rightfully belong to the Hopis."

Grandpa Jake and Ranger Reid put the gold coins they had left behind into a large knapsack and put the tomahawks in another. The arrowheads went into the third. Even though the hole in the cave was now empty, they covered it up with rocks. The wanted to be sure that if anyone else found this place, they'd find it looking just like it did ages ago.

"Okay, Cowboy Little and Cowboy Small," said Grandpa Jake, "do you recollect what you did when we left the cave the last time?"

"Yes, sir," said Cowboy Small. "We need to find some branches to cover up our tracks real good."

As they headed down Humphrey's Peak for the last time, the boys looked back. "Did you ever imagine we'd really find the treasure?" Cowboy Small asked his brother.

"No way," said Cowboy Little. "I jist wanted to find some arrowheads, and we sure enough did that!" As they brushed out their tracks, the boys hummed "Oh, Susannah," one of the tunes Cowboy José played over and over.

They loaded up the pack mule, packed their saddlebags, and got up on their horses. Grandpa Jake, Ranger Reid, Cowboy José, Cowboy Slim, Cowboy Little, Cowboy Small, their dogs Red and Fred, their fleas Itch and Scratch, and their cattle Brawny Bull, Helen Heifer, and the pack mule headed toward the Hopi village. They wanted to give Chief Tocho the arrowheads carved by their ancestors.

This time when they rode up, the braves led them right to Chief Tocho, who invited them to share another meal around the campfire.

"We came to thank you for helping us find the old huntin' cave," said Ranger Reid. "The boys found a pile of ancient arrowheads behind the rocks you described. We thought your tribe should have them."

The chief gathered the elders around him. They passed the sack of arrowheads from one to the other. Cowboy Little and

Cowboy Small could see the wonder on their faces. Later, the boys scampered off to find their friends.

After eating a hearty meal of venison and corn, Chief Tocho took Ranger Reid and Grandpa Jake aside. "We kin tell by the markings that the arrowheads were carved during my great-great-grandfather's time on earth. They are very sacred to the Hopi people. I want to thank you for bringing them to us."

He pointed to Cowboy Little and Cowboy Small, who were laughing with the Indian children. "I have no way to repay you for the arrowheads. Perhaps the little cowboys could come stay in the village for a time and learn our ways. Your boys could help our children with their English, and my grandsons could teach them our language and how to hunt with bows and arrows."

"That's a mighty fine invite, Chief Tocho," said Grandpa Jake. "We'll sure 'nuff talk it over with their mama and daddy."

Once again, the Circle R cowboys built a campsite down river from the village. When Grandpa Jake told the boys they had been invited to come back to the Hopi village for a spell, they danced a jig around the campfire.

Sleep came easy that night. The little cowboys dreamed of returning to the Hopi village to see their new friends, learn sign language, and shoot arrows with bows.

Early the next morning, they saddled up and headed back to the Circle R. The boys chattered about the arrowheads and how jealous their friends would be. Grandpa Jake and Ranger Reid tried to come up with some ideas they could suggest to

Daddy about putting the treasure to good use. They reckoned the coins were worth more than all the biggest ranches in these parts put together.

Chapter 11

CHARITY BEGINS AT HOME

Mama was mighty happy to see her boys safe and sound back at the Circle R. Cowboy Little and Cowboy Small unsaddled all the horses and put them out to pasture with Brawny Bull and Helen Heifer. While they were gone, Mama, Daddy, Grandpa Jake, Grandma Hettie, and Ranger Reid sat around the fireplace talking about the fortune.

"The boys said the schoolhouse needs a new roof, so we could help with that," said Daddy. "But I don't want to show off or do anything that will make people think we found a lot of money. There'd be no peace around here, just a lineup of folks wanting to borrow or steal it from us."

"Besides, the Whiskey Still Gang would know for sure that we had the coins and make a turrable ruckus," said Grandpa Jake.

"Of course, you git a big re-ward, Ranger Reid," said Daddy. "Without you knowing Chief Tocho, we'd 'a never found the cave. But let's ponder on what to do with the rest for a few days. Tomorrow, we need to ride into town and put the rest of the coins in the bank's strong box. I'm thankful no one besides us and two cowhands knows what we found."

After everyone else had fallen asleep, Daddy and Mama stayed up talking. "Grandpa Jake and Grandma Hettie have a big mortgage on this farm," said Mama. "Every month they worry about havin' enough money to pay the bank. Maybe we could pay the mortgage off. Then they'd never be fearful they'd lose their land and everything they've worked so hard for."

Daddy planted a big kiss on her cheek. "I think that's a dandy idea," he said. "There'll be plenty left to do some good in the town without showing off."

The next morning, Daddy and Mama rounded up Grandpa Jake, Grandma Hettie, and the four brothers. Daddy poured everyone a cup of steaming-hot coffee and sat down at the kitchen table. "Okay, family," he said. "We need to make some decisions about the fortune we found. Mama and I talked about it last night."

The little cowboys were all ears.

"First, you need to understand that these treasures don't really belong to us," said Daddy. "The arrowheads belong to the Hopi Indians, and the coins belong to the people of this territory. Your mama and I think they need to be somewhere folks kin see and read about them and the two little cowboys who found the treasure."

"How're we gonna do that?" asked Cowboy Little.

"Here's my plan," said Daddy. "We believe we should take the Spanish breastplate and the gold coins to Governor Ordway. He'll pay us a finder's fee. That's normal in sit-i-ations like this. We'll use it to pay off the mortgage on the ranch. Then Grandpa Jake and Grandma Hettie won't ever have to worry about losing their land."

Grandma Hettie cried happy tears, and Grandpa Jake's eyes filled up a little. Then his face lit up brighter than a Western sunrise. "You have no idea what that would mean for us," he said. "We're always worried about havin' enough money to pay the mortgage. Our dream is keepin' this ranch in the family for generations. Paying off the bank note will make that wish come true."

"What will the governor do with the map and the breast-plate?" asked Cowboy Small.

"He'll probably put it in his big office at the territorial cap-itol. But I think we should let him decide. We'll ask him to set up an anonymous trust to benefit Johnsonville."

"What's that word, 'anoymoose'?" asked Cowboy Small.

"That means it's a secret and no one but us will know where the money come from," Daddy said, "especially not the Whis-key Still Gang." He looked at his boys. "Mama and I are mighty proud of you all. And you should be mighty proud of your-selves, too."

Cowboy Little looked at Cowboy Small. Cowboy Small looked at Cowboy Little. They were plumb flumbustered. They didn't know what to think about Daddy and Mama's idea.

"Well," said Cowboy Little, "we've been thinking about the money, too, like we want to buy new saddles and boots for us—and some for Cowboy Big and Cowboy Tall, too. And we want to git Mama and Grandma Hettie some purty material to sew new dresses, and new chaps for Daddy and Grandpa Jake. We wouldn't have to keep much."

"Yes, indeedy, Cowboy Little and Cowboy Small," said Daddy. "Since you found it, I think you should buy somethin' special for your own selves. Thank you for thinkin' of everyone else in the family. I already gave Ranger Reid a reward for helpin' us."

All of a sudden, Cowboy Big stood up. "How're we gonna git all the coins and the breastplate to the governor without the Whiskey Still Gang comin' after us?"

"I talked to Ranger Reid before he rode off at sunup," said Daddy. "He thought we should send a wire and ask Governor Ordway to send some men from the cavalry. They could fetch the coins from the bank and take them back to the territorial capitol. I don't reckon the Whiskey Still Gang will mess with the United States Army Calvary. Those boys kin be mighty rough when it comes to fightin'.

"Then it's settled," said Daddy. "I'll go into town tomorrow with Cowboy Big and Cowboy Tall to put the rest of the coins in the bank's strong box. We'll also see how we go about payin' off the loan on the Circle R. But remember, boys. You can't tell none of your friends about this. Not ever! It's our family secret. I want you to tell me you understand," he said sternly.

Cowboy Little and Cowboy Small nodded solemnly, then they ran outside whoopin' and hollerin'. Since they could never tell any human friends, they shared the news with Ned and Ted. Then they gave each an apple so they'd know something special happened at the Circle R that day.

The boys saddled up Ned and Ted, and with their dogs Red and Fred, their fleas Itch and Scratch, and their cattle Brawny Bull and Helen Heifer tagging behind, they went for a rollicking ride 'round the ranch.

Chapter 12

AMBUSH AT THE GULCH

A few weeks later, eight soldiers from the cavalry rode up to Circle R Ranch. The captain stayed at the ranch house with the family. The rest bedded down in the bunkhouse. The next day, Daddy, Grandpa Jake, Cowboy Little, Cowboy Small, Cowboy Big, and Cowboy Tall rode with them to the Johnsonville Bank. They loaded the treasure into the wagon for the long ride to the capital.

No one noticed Sourpuss Jones peeking out from behind the saloon. When he saw the posse leave, he limped as fast as he could back to the livery stable where the Whiskey Still Gang was bedding down. "Git goin', you lazy bums!" Sourpuss yelled. "They're movin' the gold. We got to fig'er how we're gonna take it back. Times 'a wastin'!"

"Settle down," said Thurman Roundtree. "First we need to fig'er out which way they're headed. If they play it safe, they'll go south where there ain't no good ambush sites, but it'd take 'em a half-day longer. If'n they go north, they'll pass through Dry Creek Gulch, where the river used to come through. That'd be faster, but more dangerous 'cause it's a good place for an ambush. Still, I'll bet everyone a pint of sarsaparilla that's the route they take."

"But there's eight soldiers plus Daddy Randall, the big brothers, and the two rotten boys that stole our gold coins. I'm purty sure every last one is a good shot," said Sourpuss Jones. "That makes only six of us ag'in all of them."

Some of the men began grumbling.

"Do y'all want this gold or not?" shouted Thurman Roundtree. "You kin be cowards and stay behind, or come with us. But one thing's dang sure—you ain't gittin' a share if'n you stay a'bed."

After a heated argument, all six climbed on their horses. They were in luck; it had rained the night before, so the tracks of the cavalry wagon and the soldiers' horses were easy to follow. Thurman Roundtree had rightly figured the posse was headed toward the state capital by way of Dry Creek Gulch.

Determined to set up a trap to steal the gold, the Whiskey Still Gang galloped faster than the wind so they could arrive at the gulch first. And because traveling by wagon is slower than on horseback, they reached the gulch first.

"I'll say this, fellas," Thurman Roundtree said. "When you have a mind to git a move on, you sure can do it."

Thurman Roundtree told the others to stand guard. Then he galloped through the gulch to the other side and made a circle around the back to stake it out. "This here is a great spot for an ambush," he said. "Here's the plan. Sourpuss, you take two men and climb up on that bluff over yonder. The rest of us will take the opposite side."

But the gang members were not the only ones thinking about an ambush at the gulch. The captain of the cavalry was, too. As the Randalls and the soldiers got closer, he said, "Sergeant, take five men and scout out the gulch to see if we're headin' into trouble."

Before the sergeant could spot the Whiskey Still Gang, Thurman Roundtree spotted them. "Stop right thar!" he yelled from the top of the bluff. "We got you covered. Give us the gold and everybody goes home alive."

"You're welcome to go on home. But you sure don't git no gold," said the sergeant. "I guess we've got a standoff, unless you come out and fight like men. Or do you want us to come git you?"

Then the sergeant whispered to his men, "Corporal, I'll distract that blowhard leader of theirs. You sneak up behind the outlaws hidin' behind those rocks on the left side of the gulch. Take 'em by surprise and tie 'em up. Then we kin deal with the three on the other side."

The plan worked. The soldiers crept up behind Sourpuss and his sorry friends and caught them by surprise. The corporal cocked his gun. "Put your rifles down real slow-like," he ordered. "Now take off your pistol belts. Then git down on your knees."

Sourpuss Jones and the two other bandits ranted and raved. They had gotten caught in the trap they set! The soldiers tied their hands behind their backs and lassoed their feet so they couldn't get away.

Then the corporal stood behind a boulder and yelled to

Thurman Roundtree, "It looks like your boys got company over here! We got 'em hog-tied. Y'all want to come talk about what we should do with 'em?"

Thurman Roundtree was madder than a wild bull at a rodeo. He stomped and he fussed and he cussed. "Sourpuss Jones!" he yelled. "How did you git bamboozled a'gin? First you lose the saddlebags. Then you let yourself git caught by some sorry soldiers!"

"Time's runnin' out," yelled the corporal. "I'm guessing you want to keep these boys company in jail."

Thurman Roundtree turned to his buddies hiding with him on the other side of the gulch. "Boys, if'n we want to save our own skins, we best skedaddle. We're outgunned, we're outmanned, and we've been outwitted. But by gum, we'll fig'er out a way to git that gold yet."

With that, they snuck down the back side of the gulch to where they had left their horses and galloped toward their hideout near Johnsonville.

Sourpuss Jones yelled after them, "You yellow-bellied cowards! Are you jist gonna leave us here without defendin' us?"

The hog-tied outlaws got nary an answer.

With the gold still safe in the wagon and the cavalry leading the way, the group headed toward the territory capital. Just about the time the capitol dome came into view, a soldier rode toward them and saluted the captain.

"Governor Ordway sent me to lead you straight to the capitol building," he said. "Foller me."

Daddy, Cowboy Little, Cowboy Small, Cowboy Big, and

Cowboy Tall followed. Next came the eight soldiers and the three Whiskey Still bandits on horseback with their hands tied behind their backs.

When they got to the base of the capitol steps, Cowboy Little and Cowboy Small could hardly believe their eyes. "Have you ever seen such a big buildin', Daddy?"

"Hush," Daddy said gently. "Here comes the governor hisself."

"Welcome," said Governor Ordway. "I'm mighty proud to make the acquaintance of the Randall family." He shook everyone's hand, even Cowboy Little's and Cowboy Small's. The boys felt very proud.

The governor pointed to Sourpuss Jones and his two buddies. He said to the captain, "Looks like you brought me three thievin' members of the Whiskey Still Gang. I'm guessin' they tried to ambush you and steal the gold."

"Yes, sir," said the captain, saluting.

"Well, I reckon you need to find these crooks a cell at the jail," said Governor Ordway. "I have a feelin' they'll be locked up for a long time."

The Randall family followed the governor into his office. It was the fanciest place any of them had ever seen. A big map of the territory and pictures of the president of the United States and the governor himself hung on the walls. There were two rawhide sofas and a great big desk. The boys couldn't stop gawking.

"Fellas," the governor said, "the people of the territory are grateful for your generous gifts of the gold coins and Spanish breastplate. There's a big re-ward coming your way for your honesty. And the good folks in Johnsonville will be thankful for the new roof on the school and books for the library you wanted."

Daddy stepped forward. "Governor, if you don't mind, we'd appreciate it if no one knows where the money come from. It would only stir up trouble. We'd 'druther it come di-rectly from you as a gift to the citizens of Johnsonville."

Governor Ordway nodded. "I understand your thinkin'," he said.

"We sure thank you for sending the cavalry to guard the gold coins on the journey here," said Daddy. "The Whiskey Still Gang would surely have gotten the best of us at the gulch. And thank you fer invitin' us to your office. But I reckon it's time for us to mosey on back to the Circle R so we kin relax some."

"Don't relax too much on the way back," warned the governor. "What's left of the Whiskey Still Gang may seek revenge. Y'all be careful."

Instead of heading for the ranch directly, Daddy, Cowboy Big, Cowboy Tall, Cowboy Little, and Cowboy Small spent the night at the boarding house. They ate pot roast for dinner and had a breakfast of biscuits and ham. Then they headed home.

"I'm thinkin' we need to take the governor's advice," said Daddy. "Let's go the long way around. Thurman Roundtree may be hiding at the gulch just waitin' to git us for good."

It was a wise decision. As the sun slipped behind the horizon, they galloped safe and sound onto the Circle R Ranch. When they gathered around the table to eat Mama's fresh apple pie, Daddy took off his holster and hung it on the nail on the wall where he usually kept it.

"Mama, you got any fresh coffee heatin' up on the stove?" he asked.

She smiled and rose from her chair. Mama had one foot in the kitchen when she heard the floorboards squeak. She froze in her tracks. Big as you please, there was Thurman Roundtree smack dab inside their ranch house. He stepped forward and pointed his rifle at Daddy.

"Whoa there," said Daddy. "You ain't gonna shoot me in front of my missus and young'uns, are you?"

"Not today. But I'm givin' you a warnin'. You best look over your shoulder from now on out, 'cause I'm comin' fer you," said Thurman Roundtree.

Before anyone could say another word, he disappeared out the back door as silently as he'd come in. They all talked at once and Mama sniffled a little.

"Calm down, everyone," Daddy said. "I reckon his bark is worse than his bite. Otherwise he'd have used that gun on all of us. I ain't goin' after him in the dark. I'd 'druther pick my own time and my own place. But in the meantime, I'm posting guards around the ranch house at night."

After a while, Mama shooed the boys off to bed. "Y'all have had enough excitement for the day," she said.

Once they were in their bunks, Cowboy Little said, "'Cept for Thurman Roundtree scarin' us all to death, we've had a mighty fine day."

"Yep," said Cowboy Small. "I reckon we did somethin' real

special. With the money from the gold coins, the school will git a new roof and the library will git more books. And we'll have enough to buy everyone a nice present. But best of all, Grandpa Jake and Grandma Hettie kin pay off the ranch."

"We'll never have a better adventure than this one," said Cowboy Little as he snuggled into his bunk bed with Red on the floor beside him.

"Don't be too sure," said Cowboy Small. "I got a new idea rollin' 'round in my head. After we do our chores tomorrow, let's go see if there really are dancin' otters at Fiddlin' Creek. Ned and Ted, Red and Fred, Itch and Scratch, and Brawny Bull and Helen Heifer will be mighty tickled to come along."

GLOSSARY

Chaps: Seatless leather leggings worn over pants to protect a cowboy's legs

Circle R Ranch: Home of Cowboy Little, Cowboy Small, and their family

Corral: Fenced-in area for animals

Cowboy José: Pronounced "Hozay"

Cowponies: Sturdy horses that were the cowboys' best friends

Fig'er: Figure out

Grub: Food

Guffawed: Laughed

Gulch: A narrow passage along a dry creek bank with steep sides

Hankered: Wanted

Lasso: Lo-o-o-ng rope used to round up steers

Moseyed: Walked slowly

Passel: A lot of something

Pine torches: Dry pine-tree roots filled with sap that burn brightly when lit

Rifle: Gun used for hunting

Six-shooter: Gun carried in a holster that was used for protection

Saddlebags: Leather bags that held needed items on the trail

Slicker: Huge yellow oilskin overcoat and raincoat that protected the cowboy and his horse from snow and rain

Vittles: Food

Whiskey Still Gang: A group of mean cowboys or bandits known for their dishonest ways, including fighting, rustling cattle and horses, and robbing people at gunpoint

AVAILABLE SOON!

The Adventures of Cowboy Little and Cowboy Small

The Dancing Otters of Fiddlin' Creek and Other Stories

On a beautiful spring day, Cowboy Little and Cowboy Small, their dogs Red and Fred, their horses Ned and Ted, their fleas Itch and Scratch, and their cattle Brawny Bull and Helen Heifer go searching for the Dancing Otters of Fiddlin' Creek. When Sly Fox tries to make mischief, the boys fear the otters are goners. Then one of their friends comes to the rescue!

Can you guess which one?

ABOUT THE AUTHOR

Jim Rhoden is the Founder, Chairman, and Principal Owner of Futren Hospitality, which owns and manages private clubs and golf clubs in the greater Atlanta area. Throughout his long career, he has developed and managed major real estate projects in Florida, Georgia, and North Carolina, and believes strongly in giving back to his community.

He is also a talented and prolific storyteller who has amused two generations of kids with tales about his favorite characters, Cowboy Little and Cowboy Small, who love to explore the world around them.

Collaborator Mickey Goodman is a veteran memoirist, ghostwriter, and journalist with more than seven hundred by-lined articles in scores of national and regional publications. She has also coauthored five books.

ABOUT THE ILLUSTRATOR

Marilena Perilli has enjoyed working as an illustrator for over fifteen years. She has illustrated books and created artwork for numerous national brands, as well as the *New York Times*.